GROMMIT
the Vulture

A tale from a Caribbean Cockpit

Andy Campbell

MACMILLAN
CARIBBEAN

Dedication

This book is dedicated to my sister-in-law, Barbie Jardine, who rescued Grommit as a fledgling.

Yes, she actually looked after him and raised him as an 'extended member of the family'. No one knew how he would turn out, and everyone expected that one day he would fly off. How wrong we all were!

It was this close bond of friendship and caring that motivated me to write this story, albeit from Grommit's heart and soul.

Macmillan Education
Between Towns Road, Oxford OX4 3PP
A division of Macmillan Publishers Limited
Companies and representatives throughout the world

www.macmillan-caribbean.com

ISBN 0 333 98818 3

Text © Andy Campbell 2005
Illustrations © Vanessa Soodeen 2005
Design © Macmillan Publishers Limited 2005

First privately published in STORIES FROM THE COCKPIT
First published 2005

Designed by Holbrook Design Oxford Ltd
Illustrated by Vanessa Soodeen
Cover design by Holbrook Design Oxford Ltd
Cover illustration by Vanessa Soodeen

Printed and bound in Thailand

2009 2008 2007 2006 2005
10 9 8 7 6 5 4 3 2 1

ALL OF US VULTURES are born and raised in a nest on the ground. My parents chose a wonderful spot in between the protective roots of a banyan tree, half way up Lady Chancellor Hill, a stone's throw above the road.

The roots of the tree grow downwards from the limbs and create a natural protective barrier on the ground. This makes a perfect nesting area for the likes of us.

It was always comforting to know that we had some protection, although that wasn't really necessary, as vultures are never on any predator's menu. In fact, corbeaux, as we are known in Trinidad, are never considered a source of food for either man or beast. We have no natural enemies. This was very good news for a young fledgling corbeau like me.

It was all so exciting when my eyes finally started to open, like those of my brothers and sisters. During the day, when our parents were at work on environmental projects, our play in the nest used to be non-stop.

One day our 'rough-housing' got a little out of hand. Then, unfortunately, I lost my balance, rolled out of the nest backwards, tumbled all the way down to the road and sustained serious injuries. My skull was cut and my eye injured and it was in this dreadful condition and location that I remained – until I was finally saved by an angel.

In my predicament, I would not have survived very much longer, as medical facilities amongst us corbeaux leave a lot to be desired. At this point the angel appeared, picked me up and took me to her flat in a town house further up the hill.

I knew instantly that it was the sort of accommodation to which I could easily become accustomed. The view was excellent, panoramic, taking in most of Port of Spain. Inside, everything was clean and tidy, and I presumed the food would be of an equally high standard. I was surprised to find that all the perishables were kept in a large upright closet with two doors. The larger door was for the 'fridge', the smaller for the 'freezer', the section I was interested in. I personally did not like the fridge, I found it an unnecessary luxury – there is really no need to keep meat fresh. But the freezer contained a treasure trove of frozen meats, including tenderloin steaks and chicken parts.

Having just moved in to the flat, I did not want to appear too precocious and push my luck, so there I remained, contentedly, being nursed by my saviour. She was most attractive and wore stunning clothes and jewellery, and it was only after she was visited by some of her friends that I heard them call her 'Barbie'. Because I was never formally introduced to her, I continued to refer to her as 'Angel'. That was what she was to me.

Her medical care and attention were excellent, far better than I would have received in the corbeaux environment, and I was soon happily on the way to a full recovery.

Naturally, I missed my family, but the luxury of Angel's flat was more than compensation. It was what I later discovered my family called 'a sponge cake scene'. I'll explain later what that means. I was discovering new culinary delights. A corbeau's palate, of course, is accustomed to raw meat that might be days or weeks old, but now, at my new address, I was being hand-fed with fresh meat. Some of it was actually cooked!

It seemed that I was literally living in heaven with my 'Angel Barbie'. I would never let on that certain things about living at my new address were a bit annoying.

You see, corbeaux are very sophisticated creatures, highly cultured and reserved. We never whistle or squawk, and we wear our smooth black feathers like an elegantly pressed evening suit. But living with me at my new address was Mack, a rather uncouth macaw, who continually made a racket. The colours that Mack wore were gaudy and completely out of place in such elegant surroundings. Mack just did not have the culture or upbringing to be living with Angel and myself. Even his diet was unsociable. He ate every imaginable type of nut, and drank boring bowls of water.

I, on the other hand, as I have said, ate the same as Angel: steak or chicken. She fed it all to me by hand. I knew that Angel was probably in love with me. That was perfectly understandable, given my good looks and suave manner. Poor Mack, he just did not belong, and, coupled with all his shortcomings, he had a huge beak that was far too large for his face.

As time went on, I grew from strength to strength, thanks to Angel and her undivided attention. I think that she was also beginning to realise how uncultured Mack was, or, to put it a different way, maybe she was beginning to appreciate my true sophistication. What a great catch I was!

One day, when Angel was busy at her workbench, I strutted through the house to have a closer look at what she was doing. Just before I reached her side, out of the corner of my eye I caught sight of a truly beautiful creature. I had to get a closer look, and as I approached the beauty, it too came closer to me. I slowly moved my head sideways to focus one eye properly. At exactly the same time, the gorgeous creature made the same move.

I soon realised that I was looking at myself in a mirror! It was the first time that I had ever seen myself and I was not disappointed.

I saw a streamlined and functional beak and a jet-black head, with firm, youthful good looks, trimmed with shiny, ebony feathers to match my crown. I was obviously very handsome and this made me blush a little, whenever I looked in the mirror, but Angel never detected this, as I was now perched next to her, admiring her work.

She obviously cared very much for me, as all the beautiful rings that she was working on were exactly my size. I could wear them either on my feet as pigeons do, or, perhaps around my neck. The problem was that I just didn't know how she intended to put them in place, but I would leave that up to her to sort out.

Poor Mack, he was so jealous when he saw me walking graciously round the flat. Every time he tried to do the same, he would almost trip over. He was typically parrot-toed and clumsy.

Angel had a very good friend who lived in the flat downstairs. Her name was Rachel. She was also a jeweller and she made some very attractive pieces. I just could not believe my luck! Two of the most beautiful women that I have ever seen were both making jewellery just for me.

I was recently christened 'Grommit'. Rachel said it rhymed with 'vomit'. I did not know exactly what it meant but I thought it sounded rather stylish.

As time progressed, I would perch on my balcony and observe my distant cousins circling overhead, soaring for hours on a sunny day. I decided it was time to learn to fly. Each day I would stay perched and flap my wings continuously, until I was sufficiently confident to make my first solo flight. However, I have to admit that I was just not brave enough to leap off the balcony into the valley below, so I decided first to practise indoors.

Up the semi-circular steps I climbed. From the first floor, I would have a perfect glide path in line for a soft landing on Angel's couch. I planned to extend my wings to the maximum and then simply try my first glide.

The ideal time was when Angel was out shopping. Her two lazy dogs were sleeping in the yard and, best of all, Mack was in his cage and would not be able to see my first attempt at flight. I could not go through the embarrassment of him seeing if by any unfortunate chance I failed! Only the previous week, I had given him a long lecture on how ungainly the flying style of macaws and parrots was in contrast to that of corbeaux, who can soar for hours without having to flap our wings. If anything went wrong, it would give him something to squawk about for weeks!

With wings outstretched and head down, I took one last look at my flight path and dived off in the direction of Angel's soft couch. My eyes stayed fixed on the couch and in a split second I realised that something had gone dreadfully wrong.

The couch was not getting any closer, but the wooden floor was rapidly approaching! I changed the angle of attack of my wings and desperately started flapping backwards to break my fall.

It was too little, too late! I landed squarely on Angel's coffee table, capsizing all her beautiful silver picture frames in the process. I skidded on over the edge of the table and landed head first on the ground.

What a disaster!

Fortunately, I wasn't injured and I had a quick look in the mirror. My good looks were still intact.

It would be impossible to place the picture frames upright, using only my beak, so I hurriedly picked up the loose feathers that had been torn from my chest on impact and quickly retired to the balcony. I was very fortunate that Mack hadn't, in fact, witnessed the fiasco – he would still be laughing!

Just as I was thinking about my good luck, Rachel came rushing in. She had heard all the commotion from downstairs. She went straight to the coffee table and tidied everything, mumbling something about 'It must have been a strong gust of wind!'

What a stroke of luck! No-one had discovered my first flying disaster. Learning to fly indoors was definitely not the way to go. For my next attempt, I would just have to go 'cold turkey', dive off the balcony and hope for the best.

For days, I agonised about my first solo flight. In my heart I knew I could do it, but there was always the slim possibility of failure, and this, for me, would mean death!

The following week I finally decided the time had come. I cautiously climbed onto the top rung of the balcony and gripped it tightly with my sweaty talons. For the first time in my life I had started to sweat. My pulse was racing, my breathing became short, and I was truly scared as many thoughts raced through my mind. The most terrifying was, if I failed, what would happen to me?

As I thought of possible death, I could clearly see the local paupers' graveyard in the valley below. Its untidy landscape, with gravestones and crosses randomly placed, was a most forbidding sight, and yet I still did not know if the likes of myself would qualify for burial in such a place.

Finally I could wait no more. The time had come and the moment was now!

I crouched lower, then sprang off the balcony, head first, diving towards what could be my final resting place. The rush of air over my sweating head was most comforting, but what was frightening was the speed at which the paupers' graveyard was getting closer.

I continued diving until my air speed increased sufficiently to glide, then, one or two gentle flaps and I was on my way into the wild blue yonder.

As I practised day after day, I quickly got the hang of soaring, using hot air thermals to provide lift. On a sunny day, I could stay airborne for hours without having to flap my wings. I knew that Mack was watching me closely and that he would be green with envy about my achievement! He would never be able to do this himself and, on the few occasions I saw him attempting to flap, he was clearly badly co-ordinated.

While soaring, I met dozens of other corbeaux. In conversation with them I came to realise how very special we are. I already knew about our good looks and smooth appearance, but it was only now that I found out about our vital place in the world.

All corbeaux are employed full-time with the Ministry of Environmental Affairs. Amongst our species we can boast 100% employment, as everyone has a permanent job in cleaning up the environment. We are all classified as 'Sanitary Inspectors First Class', and further sub-divided into more detailed divisions. The corbeaux who patrol the highways are in the 'Canine and Feline Division'. This division is the most senior and it is busiest at first morning light; even more so on Saturdays and Sundays. The extra traffic on the roads at weekends creates many casualties amongst stray dogs and cats. Corbeaux seldom fly at night as it is considered hazardous, and the latest union agreement only allows work during daylight hours. The net result is that the early morning shift at weekends is very busy, especially after long holidays and over the Carnival season. Occasionally, extra sanitary inspectors are brought in from other divisions.

The group that works at the 'La Basse' garbage dump are the 'Garbologist Inspectors' and they are the next senior division. They have a wider selection of food, but frequently complain that they never know what is on the menu. The competition at this location is very keen, so they have to swallow their food in a most undignified manner. Failure to do so results in some other scavenger getting the morsel. So the 'La Basse Division' are forced to eat meals far too quickly and, as a result, the garbologist inspectors suffer from chronic indigestion and constant flatulence.

The group that circles over forested areas is in charge of the 'Wildlife and Forestry Division' and comprises the more junior interns. This is the least rewarding job, as food is scarce. Little wildlife is ever found dead.

There is also a small division on the east coast that works for the 'Fisheries Division'. It can sometimes get quite busy for them, just after a large fishing seine has been brought ashore.

Unfortunately, the competition for the leftover fish is severe. The fishermen are always most inconsiderate and take all the good fish for themselves, leaving all the bony, unpalatable fish for the corbeaux attached to the 'Fisheries Division'.

These corbeaux have further problems with illegal competition from unlicensed stray dogs in the area. The dogs have cleverly re-classified themselves as 'Man's Best Friend' and, as Man includes fishermen, this means that dogs are more socially accepted than corbeaux in the midst of discarded fish. So there are fewer fish for us corbeaux and at our next union meeting this problem will have to be addressed. Naturally, the Trinidad Society for the Prevention of Cruelty to Animals has to get involved and come down to Mayaro to catch these unlicensed critters.

I came to realise that we corbeaux, apart from being attractive, are unquestionably the most useful birds in the universe. It was no wonder that Angel had rescued me as an infant. Many of the vultures that I had met on that first day's flight invited me to join their flock, but obviously I was obliged to decline in a gracious manner; Angel just could not live without me. Besides, I was sure that my accommodation and food were far superior to theirs. I have become quite accustomed to sitting at a proper table and being hand-fed by Angel, but all this would cease if I changed my address.

Recently, I had started to enjoy watching television with Angel at

my side. I shall always remember one memorable cowboy movie that I saw. It had a corbeau in a starring role.

The cowboy was seriously injured and for many days was very close to death in a lonely desert. Keeping a constant watch over him was a very caring vulture that continued to circle overhead until the injured man was finally rescued by friends. It was good to see that corbeaux are being chosen for leading roles in movies, and I hoped that this trend would continue.

Nevertheless, it was a bit off-putting having Mack peeping out of his cage at Angel and myself during these tender moments. At times like these, I wished he would show some sensitivity and look the other way, or just perhaps conveniently nod off.

Every day of my life was a fresh experience and I learnt something new about Trinidad. In the morning, right after breakfast, I would take up my usual perch on the balcony, have a good look at what was going on and wait a couple of hours for the sun to get sufficiently hot. This would produce the hot air thermals that I required to stay airborne for hours. While waiting, I would see dozens of different species of birds fly by and, as usual, the parrots would be ungainly and make the most noise. Like my boisterous flatmate, Mack, they were raucous and I just knew that sooner or later this behaviour was going to get them into a lot of trouble. It didn't take me long to find out just how much trouble!

One morning, I glided down
the entire length of the valley,
following the winding direction
of the Lady Chancellor Road. It
made numerous sharp turns that
caused my head to spin violently
from side to side and this tested
my piloting skills to the limit. I
had a lot of flying experience
now, but if I kept my eyes glued
to the road, I noticed I suffered
some vertigo and my turns were
becoming unco-ordinated.
Instead of making a proper
banked turn, I was either
skidding out of the turn or side-
slipping inwards. Self-criticism
is always good in aviation
matters and it was something
that I would have to correct
in the future.

As soon as the road reached the Savannah intersection, I turned hard left and decided to land at a large detention compound called the 'Emperor Valley Zoo'. I touched down alongside a huge cage that contained a number of macaws, not unlike Mack. In addition to ones like him, with the gaudy blue and yellow mix, there were also ones with a brighter red and blue combination. They were terribly attired, with no dress sense! And their screeching! Presumably, they had been found guilty of disturbing the peace and so incarcerated in the Zoo.

The word 'Zoo' obviously means a detention centre for minor offences. It must be a sort of half-way house for creatures who have committed misdemeanours.

In a cage nearby was an assortment of parrots who had obviously been convicted of the same offence, disturbing the peace. In addition to this, some of them must have been doing extra time for praedial larceny, as we had reports from the 'Wildlife and Forestry Division' that parrots had been observed destroying farmers' crops.

I just knew that there must be a place such as this. It confirmed my suspicion that the noisy and unruly behaviour of parrots and such like could not go unpunished.

A couple of cages further on, there was an enormous macajuel snake who had been caught stealing, thanks to his own stupidity. What I heard was that, late one night, he had slithered into a chicken farm and had swallowed a large fowl. He was then so large it was impossible for him to make good his escape through the wire mesh. The following morning, the furious chicken farmer arrested the snake, catching him red-handed, with the evidence clearly showing in his distended stomach. Stealing chickens was a fairly serious charge and I guessed the average fowl thief might be in for at least three months.

What was very obvious at the Zoo was that not a single corbeau was detained, a testimony to what I have said all along: we are law-abiding, fully employed birds, making an honest living with the Ministry of Environmental Affairs.

Recently, I was gratified to discover a law on the statute books that prevents anyone from destroying, maiming or attempting to eradicate any of my species. So even the authorities are aware of our importance. On the other hand, they obviously kept a close eye on the trouble-makers, parrots and macaws. Poor Mack, he never knew how close he was to being charged with a misdemeanour and incarcerated in the Zoo!

One of the largest group of offenders was the monkeys. In the bush they had no respect for fruit trees and farmers' cultivations, and they obviously were in the 'big house', doing serious time. It was my guess that the parrots and macaws might only be in for a short spell, depending on their behaviour, provided they did not squawk about too much. Life was a learning process and these creatures had to find out, just like humans, 'if you don't want to do the time, don't do the crime!'

In my privileged position, I never took part in any of the gourmet sessions that the other corbeaux indulged in during the day. I much preferred home cooking and being hand-fed by Angel, so I generally would just circle overhead and look at my friends putting in an honest, hard day's work at the La Basse and along the busy east-west corridor.

After my main course at dinner, I would sometimes be offered dessert. Recently this was sponge cake, which was quite delicious. I even went back for seconds, and it was only then that I overheard a disparaging comment by one of Angel's guests. 'I thought corbeaux doh eat spong cake!'

To hear such a classless individual speaking pidgin English in such an insulting manner was truly upsetting. What I would have liked to explain to him was that we always love to eat sponge cake, but no-one ever offers it to us.

On wet or cloudy days, at many locations on the island, corbeaux can be seen standing proudly with their wings outstretched. Our detractors frequently say that we are taking industrial action against our employers, the Government. Others claim that it is either a sick-out or protest action for better conditions. Nothing can be further from the truth. On overcast days, there are simply no hot air thermals to keep us airborne on patrol duty. The reason we stand with our wings outstretched is to keep them as dry as possible, as we are on standby duty in case of an emergency call.

Every time Angel left the flat to visit, I would easily follow the progress of her car. She, of course, never knew, as I would be at altitude, following her every move. Only last week I followed her car all the way up the North Coast Road and finally into Maracas Bay. That was pretty exciting and I met a mix of birds from various divisions there. There were a couple of corbeaux from 'Fisheries' that had recently transferred from Mayaro, and a few that normally worked at the La Basse during the week and were putting in some overtime at weekends at Maracas Bay. Once again, unlicensed stray dogs were creating severe competition. Angel never knew that I had followed her, and when she saw me with a large group of fellow corbeaux, I made no affectionate advances towards her. So she just stared in my direction and didn't recognise me. I didn't smile or acknowledge that I knew her, and because the other corbeaux were also blessed with my good looks, she never detected my presence.

At night I would sleep at the top of a telephone pole outside the flat, in a perfect spot for sentry duty. No one would ever look up the pole in the darkness and I had literally a bird's eye view of what was going on.

Corbeaux cannot whistle or squawk to raise an alarm. I guess I could maybe flap my wings in an emergency, but this problem demonstrates that even we corbeaux are sadly not perfect in all situations.

In the afternoons, when Angel and her friends went for walks up the road, I would let them get about 200 metres further on and then dive off the top of my telephone pole and glide up the road at waist level at a terrific rate of knots. As soon as I had arrived in the midst of her friends, I would deploy air brakes with maximum trailing edge feathers. This would kill the airspeed, where-upon I would fully extend both feet for a soft touch down in the middle of Angel's admiring friends.

Initially they were terrified, but on seeing my smooth landing, they would smile appreciatively. I wasn't showing off, or anything like that. It's just that it was so exhilarating flying so close to the ground and besides, I know Angel enjoyed watching my piloting skills. Recently I had logged a lot of flying hours and had become quite accomplished in aerobatics.

One of the most spectacular experiences to date happened only recently, when Angel decided to take me on vacation to Tobago. We travelled by boat, but I never got a proper cabin. I was placed in a cage, much the same as the creatures that were 'doing time' at the zoo. It was most undignified. I was treated like common cargo! However, I was going on vacation and had beautiful Tobago as my destination. I had heard all sorts of stories about Tobago, but one of the most intriguing was that there were no corbeaux on the island.

This was difficult to understand and I wondered if there was some sort of social discrimination against us, or a special reason why none of my relatives had ever prospered on this island, that was known as 'Crusoe's Island'. On the trip over, many curious onlookers asked why I was being kept as a pet, with comments such as, 'Couldn't you have found a prettier bird?'

These comments usually came from ignorant people who never looked long enough to observe my handsome features, nor did they have a clue how useful my species is.

The vacation home that Angel was staying in was quite spectacular, high above the Mount Irvine Golf Course, with an unrestricted view of Buccoo Reef in the distance. I felt at home at this new location, though I would probably get lonely if what they had been saying was true.

I soon found out when Angel opened the cage door and gave me back my freedom. I immediately glided down the hillside and soared over the golf course to investigate my new domain. It was truly a beautiful island. These were hardly any cars on the roads, and it was all very tidy and well kept.

But they were right, no other corbeaux around. Higher and higher I climbed to get a better view of the island, and at about 2000 feet the easterly air currents were very strong indeed. The wind speed was easily over 30 km/ph, which made it extremely difficult to get back to my vacation home.

I found myself being blown further and further to the west and it was such a struggle to get back that I became completely exhausted. It was only after I was safely back, perched on my verandah, that I understood why corbeaux never took up residence on Crusoe's Island. What a wind!

The other problem for corbeaux in Tobago is the scarcity of food. There are very few stray dogs or cats on that island, and there is little vehicular traffic compared to Trinidad. This all means that Tobago is not the ideal all-inclusive holiday destination for hungry corbeaux! Maybe it would be fine as a kind of health spa resort for overweight birds that are in need of exercise.

Within a couple of days I did get lonely and I longed to be with my fellow corbeaux inTrinidad. On top of that, every morning very early and in the late evening I had to put up with the annoying screeches of the cocorico birds.

I was bored in paradise now, and I decided to leave.

But I was determined not to return to Trinidad by boat, incarcerated in the same cage as before. I was determined to keep my independence. No boat for me. I can fly!

So I took off the day before we were scheduled to leave and it was the easiest flight I had ever had. I simply headed in the direction of Trinidad, and, with the strong wind taking me to the west, I ended up in Maracas Bay in two hours. There I overnighted with a couple of my friends from the 'Fisheries Department' and the following day I returned to Angel's flat just in time to welcome her home from Tobago.

It was actually quite an emotional moment, as she stood there, holding my empty cage, with tears in her eyes. She obviously thought that I had left her for good.

As for the future, many attractive lady corbeaux have made advances in my direction, and a very special one that I recently met is Clementine. Tall and graceful and extremely hard-working, she is senior in rank and works the busy intersections along the east-west corridor. I haven't yet decided if I want to settle down, but, just in case I do, Clementine will obviously have to be domesticated and learn to live indoors.

My other consideration is that I do not approve of the way corbeaux traditionally build their nests on the ground. This can be dangerous. Just remember what happened to me as an infant!
I simply do not want anything like that to happen with any of my offspring. Having given it considerable thought, I decided that the best solution might be to get married in a civil ceremony, and then Clementine would just move in and live with Angel and me.

I know if we did it this way, Angel would be heartbroken at first, at having to share me with my wife, but surely she would slowly get to accept my beautiful Clementine. Naturally we would need an area of the flat far away from Mack's prying eyes and noisy gestures. I plan eventually to have a large family and they obviously would have to be all hand-fed like myself and Clementine. I'm sure Angel would be delighted to do this.

These are my plans for the future, but, before I get involved with all this responsibility, I want to find my lost family, including my brothers and sisters. Only after I have located them and have invited them to move in with me and Angel, will it be fair to think of getting married and raising my large family. When I do, we will need about half the flat, especially the living room area, including the couch.

However, I won't make any firm commitments yet. For the time being, I will remain gracefully perched at the top of my telephone pole in the evenings. I don't usually attempt to go out at night, as I don't possess a night rating on my pilot's licence.

So if any of you people would care to visit, you can look me up. I shall always be at the top of my telephone pole at night, looking out for visitors.

Grommit's Album

Grommit and parrot

Young Grommit

Mac-the-Knife

House training

Grommit and Pumpkin

Grommit's
first bath

Grommit on
Angel's shoulder

changing angle of
attack of wings

wings flapping backwards to break fall

Soaring in thermals

Hot air currents
pushing upwards

Hot air

Airbrake (to reduce speed and altitude rapidly)

Increases drag

wing

Aileron

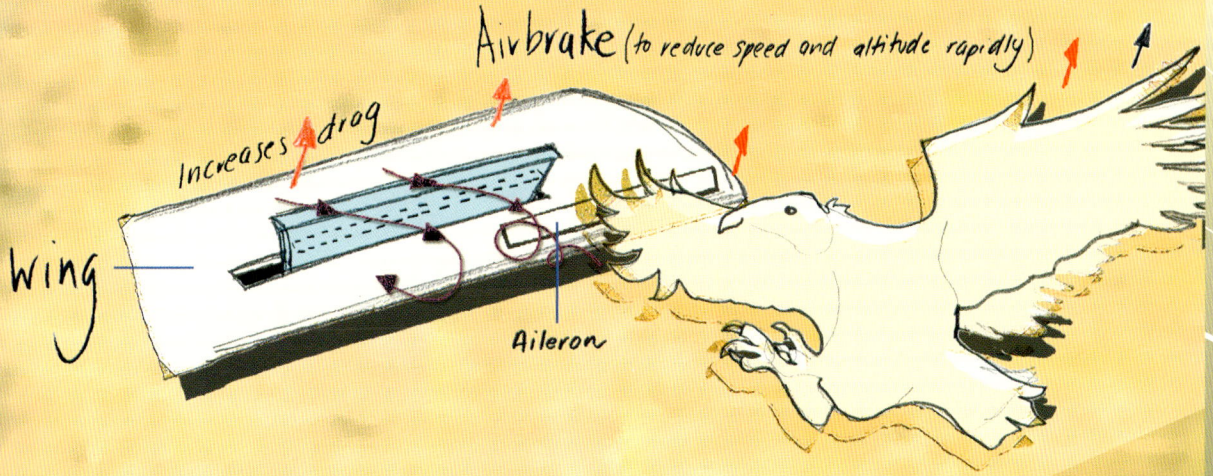

Deploying air brakes

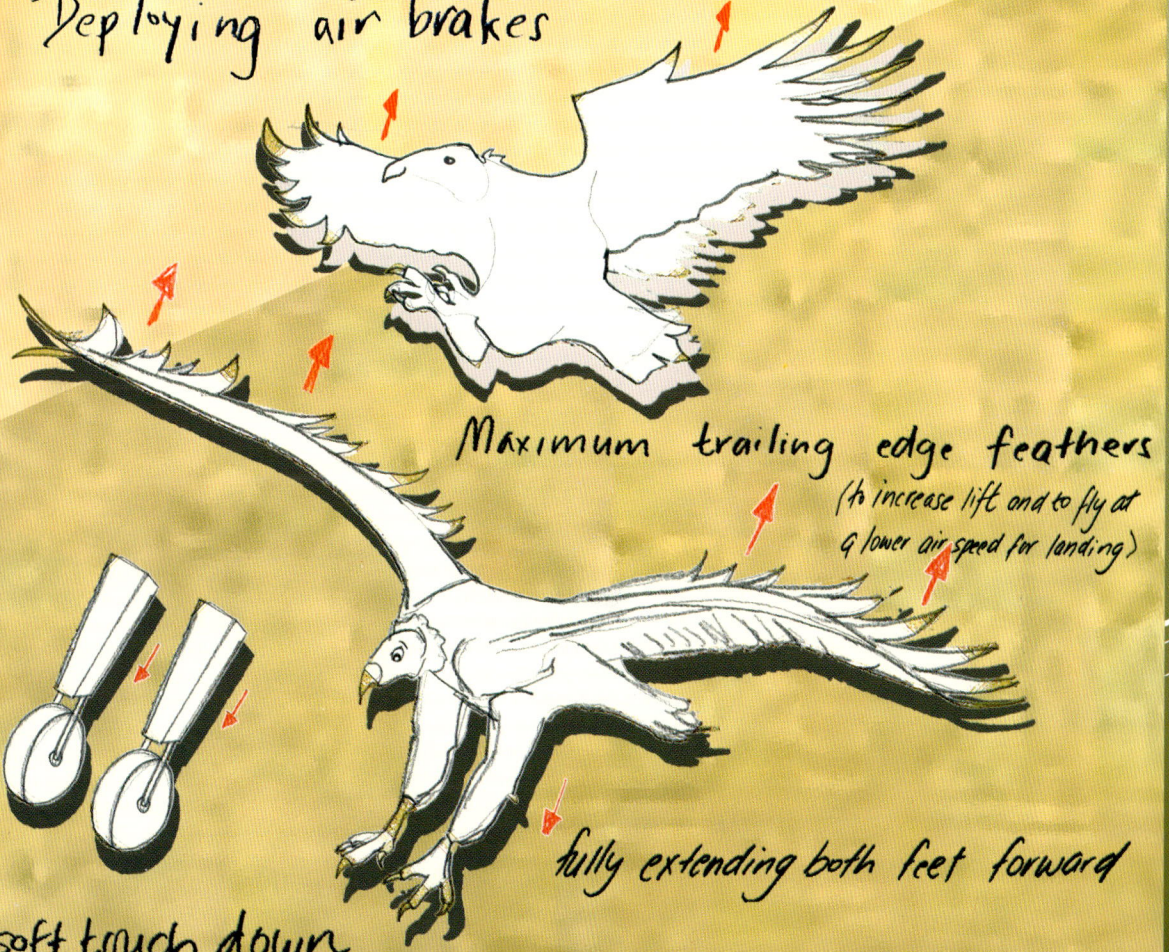

Maximum trailing edge feathers
(to increase lift and to fly at
a lower air speed for landing)

fully extending both feet forward

A soft touch down

Descent

A banked turn

A banked turn

Aileron

Aileron

θ

frontal view